Florville and Courval

(or Fatalism)

Florville and Courval

(or Fatalism)

by Marquis de Sade

Start Publishing PD LLC
Copyright © 2024 by Start Publishing PD LLC

All rights reserved, including the right to reproduce this book or portions thereof in any form whatsoever.

Start Publishing PD is a registered trademark of Start Publishing PD LLC
Manufactured in the United States of America

Cover art: Shutterstock/Taisiya Kozorez

Cover design: Jennifer Do

10 9 8 7 6 5 4 3 2 1

ISBN 979-8-8809-0473-0

Monsieur de Courval had just turned fifty-five. Vigorous and healthy, he could reasonably expect to live another twenty years. Having had nothing but unpleasantness from his first wife, who had long ago abandoned him in order to throw herself into a life of debauchery, and being obliged, on the basis of unequivocal testimony, to assume that this creature was in her grave, he began contemplating the idea of again entering into the bonds of matrimony, this time with a sensible woman who, by the kindness of her character and the excellence of her morals, would make him forget his earlier mishaps.

Unfortunate in his children as well as in his wife, he had had only two: a girl whom he had lost at a very early age, and a boy who, at the age of fifteen, had abandoned him as his wife had done, unfortunately in order to pursue the same licentious ways. Believing that nothing would ever bind him to this monster, Monsieur de Courval planned to disinherit him and bequeath all his possessions to the children he hoped to have with the new wife he wanted to take. He had an income of fifteen thousand francs a year; he had formerly been in business, and this was the fruit of his work. He was living on it in a respectable manner, with a few friends who all cherished and esteemed him, and saw him either in Paris, where he had an attractive apartment on the Rue Saint-Marc, or, more often, on a charming little estate near Nemours, where he spent two-thirds of the year.

This upright man confided his plan to his friends. When they expressed approval of it, he urged them to ask among their acquaintances to learn whether any of them knew a woman between the ages of thirty and thirty-five, either unmarried or a widow, who might fulfill his wishes.

Two days later one of his former colleagues came to tell him that he thought he had found exactly what he needed.

"The girl I'm proposing to you," this friend said to him, "has two things against her; I'll begin by telling them to you, so that I can console you afterward by describing her good qualities. It's certain that her parents are not alive, but no one knows who they were or where she lost them. All that's known is that she's a cousin of Monsieur de Saint-Prât, a reputable man who acknowledges her, holds her in great esteem, and will gladly express to you his enthusiastic and well-deserved praise of her. She has no inheritance from her parents, but Monsieur de Saint-Prât gives her four thousand francs a year. She was brought up in his house and spent her whole youth there. So much for her first fault, let's go on to her second: an affair at the age of sixteen, and a child who's no longer alive. She never seen the father again. Those are the things against her; now for a few words about those in her favor.

"Mademoiselle de Florville is thirty-six, but she looks no more than twenty-eight, it would be difficult to imagine a more pleasing and interesting face. Her features are soft and delicate, her skin has the whiteness of a lily, and her brown hair hangs down almost to her feet. Her fresh, appealing mouth is like a springtime rose. She's very tall, but she has such an excellent figure, and so much grace in her movements, that no one is unfavorably impressed by her height, which might otherwise give her a rather hard appearance. Her arms, her neck and her legs are all shapely, and she has a kind of beauty that will not grow old for a long time.

"As for her conduct, it's extreme regularity may not please you. She doesn't like social activities, and she leads a secluded life. She's very pious and very conscientious in the duties of the convent in which she lives. While she edifies everyone around her by her religious qualities, she also enchants everyone who sees her by the charms of her mind and the sweetness of her character . . . In short, she's an angel on earth, sent by heaven for the happiness of your old age."

Monsieur de Courval, delighted by this description, eagerly asked his friend to let him see the girl in question.

"I don't care about her birth," he said. "As long as her blood is pure, what does it matter who transmitted it to her? And her adventure at the age of sixteen doesn't alarm me, either: she's made up for that failing by many years of virtuous conduct. I'll simply consider that I'm marrying a widow; having decided to take a woman between thirty and thirty-five, it would have been hard for me to maintain a foolish insistence on virginity. So nothing displeases me in your proposal, and I can only urge you to let me see the object of it."

Monsieur de Courval's friend soon granted his wish: three days later he invited him to dinner with the young woman of whom he had spoken. It would have been difficult not to be enchanted at first sight by that charming girl. She had the features of Minerva herself, disguised beneath those of love. Since she knew what was at issue, she was even more reserved than usual. Her discretion, her modesty and the nobility of her bearing, combined with her many physical charms, her gentle character and her keen, well-developed mind, left poor Courval so enraptured that he begged his friend to hasten the conclusion.

He saw her several more times, in his friend's house, in his own, and in Monsieur de Saint-Prât's. Finally, in response to his earnest entreaties, she told him that nothing could be more pleasing to her than the honor he wanted to bestow on her, but that her conscience would not allow her to accept it until she herself had related the vicissitudes of her life to him.

"You haven't been told everything, monsieur," she said, "and I can't consent to be yours unless you know more about me. Your esteem is so important to me that I don't want to risk losing it, and I would certainly not deserve it if, taking advantage of your illusions about me, I were to agree to be your wife without giving you a chance to judge whether or not I'm worthy of it."

Monsieur de Courval assured her that he knew everything, that it was he, rather than she, who ought to have misgivings about his worthiness, and that if he was fortunate enough to please her, she had no reason to trouble herself about anything. But she held firm: she told him emphatically that she would not consent to anything until he had been thoroughly informed by her. He had to give in to her; all he was able to obtain from her was that she would come to his estate near Nemours, that all preparations would be made for the wedding he desired, and that she would become his wife the day after he had heard her story.

"But, monsieur," said that gracious girl, "since all those preparations may be in vain, why make them? What if I should persuade you that I'm not meant for you?"

"You'll never prove that to me, mademoiselle," replied the honest Courval. "I defy you to prove it to me. Let us go, I beg you, and don't oppose my plans."

It was impossible to make him change his mind. Everything was arranged and they went to his estate. They were alone, however, as Mademoiselle de Florville had demanded: the things she had to say were not to be revealed to anyone except the man who wanted to marry her, so no one else was admitted. The day after their arrival that beautiful and interesting girl asked monsieur de Courval to listen to her, and told him the events of her life in these words:

Mademoiselle de Florville's Story

Your intentions with regard to me, monsieur, make it imperative that you be deceived no longer. You've seen Monsieur de Saint-Prât; you've been told that I'm related to him, and he himself was kind enough to say so, and yet you were greatly deceived on that point. My family is unknown to me; I've never had the satisfaction of knowing to whom I owe my birth. A few days after I was born, I was found in a green taffeta bassinet on Monsieur de Saint-Prât's doorstep. Attached to the canopy over my bassinet was an anonymous letter which said simply:

Since you have been married for ten years without having a child and still want one every day, adopt this one. Her blood is pure: she is the fruit of a virtuous marriage, and not of debauchery; she comes from an honorable family. If she does not please you, you can have her taken to a foundling home. Do not make any inquiries, because none of them would be successful. It is impossible to tell you anything more.

I was immediately taken in by the good people at whose house I'd been left. They brought me up, took the best possible care of me, and I can say that I owe them everything. Since there was no indication of my name, it pleased Madame de Saint-Prât to name me Florville.

I had just reached the age of fifteen when I had the misfortune of seeing my foster mother die. Nothing could express the grief I felt at losing her. I had become so dear to her that just before her death she begged her husband to allot me an income of four thousand francs a year and never to abandon me. Monsieur de Saint-Prât granted these two requests. He was also kind enough to acknowledge me as a cousin of his wife and to draw up a marriage contract for me under that title, as you have seen.

He made it clear to me, however, that I could no longer stay in his house. "I'm a widower, and still young," that virtuous man said to me. "If you and I were to live under the same roof now, it would give rise to doubts which we don't deserve. Your happiness and your reputation are dear to me: I don't want to endanger either of them. We must part, Florville, but I will never abandon you as long as I live, and I don't even want you to go outside of my family. I have a widowed sister in Nancy. I'm going to send you to her. You can count on her friendship the same as mine. With her, you'll still be before my eyes, so to speak, and I can continue to take care of everything that will be required to complete your education and establish you in life."

I wept when I heard this news. It gave me an additional sorrow which bitterly renewed my grief over the death of my foster mother. But I was convinced of the soundness of Monsieur de Saint-Prât's reasoning, so I decided to follow his advice. I left for Lorraine in the company of a lady from that region to whom I had been entrusted. She brought me to Madame de Verquin, Monsieur de Saint-Prât's sister, with whom I was to live.

Madame de Verquin's house was quite different from Monsieur de Saint-Prât's. In his, I had seen decency, religion and morality reign supreme; in hers, frivolity, independence and the pursuit of pleasure were enthroned.

When I'd been there only a few days, Madame de Verquin warned me that my prudish air displeased her, that it was outrageous to come from Paris with such awkward manners and such a ridiculous strain of virtue in one's character, and that if I wanted to get along with her I'd have to adopt another tone. This beginning alarmed me. I won't try to make myself appear better than I am, monsieur, but everything contrary to morality and religion has always displeased me so intensely, I've always been so strongly opposed to anything that offends virtue, and the sins to which I've been driven in spite of myself have caused me so much remorse, that I must confess to you that you won't be rendering me a service if you bring me back into the world. I wasn't made to live in it, it makes me feel shy and morose. The deepest seclusion is what best suits the state of my soul and the inclinations of my mind.

These reflections, still badly formulated and not sufficiently ripened at such an early age, save me neither from Madame de Verquin's bad advice nor from the calamities into which her enticement was to plunge me. The constant company and hectic pleasures with which I was surrounded, the examples and words of others -- everything combined to lead me astray. I was told that I was pretty, and, unfortunately for me, I dared to believe it.

The Normandy regiment was garrisoned in Nancy at that time. Madame de Verquin's house was a meeting place for the officers. All the young women came too, and it was there that all the amorous intrigues of the town were begun, broken off and recomposed.

It was unlikely that Monsieur de Saint-Prât knew all about his sister's conduct. With his austere morality, how could he have consented to send me to her if he had known her well? This consideration held me back and prevented me from complaining to him. And, if I must confess everything, it's even possible that I had little desire to complain to him. The impure air I was breathing had begun to pollute my soul, and, like Telemachus on Calypso's island, I might not have listened to Mentor's advice.

One day the shameless Madame de Verquin, who had been trying to corrupt me for a long time, asked me whether I was sure I'd brought a pure heart with me to Lorraine, and whether I hadn't left a lover behind me in Paris.

"I've never even thought of the failings you suspect me of," I replied "and your brother will answer for my conduct . . ."

"Failings?" interrupted Madame de Verquin. "If you have one, it's being too innocent for your age. I hope you'll correct it."

"Oh, madame ! Is that the kind of language I ought to hear from such a respectable lady?"

"Respectable? Ah, not another word ! I assure you, my dear, that respect is the feeling I care least about. Love is what I want to inspire. I'm not yet old enough for respect. Follow my example, my dear, and you'll be happy. . . .By the way, have you noticed Senneval?" added that siren, referring to a seventeen-year-old officer who often came to her house.

"Not particularly," I replied. "I can assure you that I see them all with the same indifference."

"That's just what you mustn't do, my young friend. From now on, I want us to share our conquests. You must have Senneval. He's my handiwork, I've taken the trouble to develop him. He's in love with you. You must have him. . . ."

"Oh, madame, please don't insist on it ! Really, I'm not interested in anyone ! "

"You must do it: I've already made arrangements with his colonel, who's my current lover, as you've seen."

"Please leave me free to make my own choice. I'm not at all inclined toward the pleasures you cherish."

"Oh, that will change ! Some day you'll like them as much as I do. It's easy not to cherish something you don't know yet, but it's inadmissible to refuse to know something that was made to be adored. In short, the whole thing has already been planned: Senneval will declare his passion to you this evening, and I don't want you to make him wait too long before you satisfy it, otherwise I'll be angry with you--seriously angry."

At five o'clock the company gathered. Since the weather was hot, card games were organized outside in the groves. Things had been so well arranged that Monsieur de Senneval and I found that we were the only ones who were not playing cards, so we were obliged to talk with each other.

It would be pointless to conceal the fact that as soon as that charming and witty young man had told me of his love for me, I felt irresistibly drawn toward him. When I later tried to understand that attraction, I found that everything about it was obscure to me. It seemed to me that it wasn't the effect of an ordinary feeling: its characteristics were hidden from me by a veil before my eyes. On the other hand, at the very moment when my heart flew toward him, an invincible force seemed to hold it back, and in that tumult, that ebb and flow of incomprehensible ideas, I was unable to decide whether I was right to love Senneval or whether I ought to flee from him forever.

He was given ample time to confess his love to me . . . Alas, he was given too much ! I had time enough to appear responsive to him. Taking advantage of my agitation, he demanded an admission of my feelings. I was weak enough to tell him that he was far from displeasing me, and three days later I was sinful enough to let him enjoy his victory.

The malicious joy of vice in its triumphs over virtue is a truly extraordinary thing. Madame de Verquin was ecstatic when she learned that I'd fallen into the trap she'd set for me. She made fun of me, laughed at me, and finally assured me that what I'd done was the simplest, most reasonable thing in the world, and that I could receive my lover in her house every night without fear; because she would see nothing. She said she was too busy to concern herself with such trifles, but that she would admire my virtue nevertheless, because I would probably limit myself to the one lover I had just chosen, while she, lacking my modesty and reserve, had to contend with three of them at once.

When I took the liberty of telling her that such promiscuity was odious, that it presupposed neither sensitivity nor sentiment, and that it reduced our sex to the level of the vilest species of animals, she burst out laughing and said, "'Gallic heroine,' I admire you and don't blame you. I know very well that at your age sensitivity and sentiment are gods to whom one sacrifices pleasure. At my age, it's different: completely disillusioned about those phantoms, one gives them a little less power; sensual pleasures that are more real are preferred to the silly delusions that fill you with enthusiasm. Why should we be faithful to men who aren't faithful to us? Isn't it enough to be weaker without also being more gullible? A woman who has qualms about such actions is foolish . . . Take my advice, my dear: vary your pleasures while your age and your charms allow you to do it, and abandon your absurd faithfulness.

It's a gloomy, repugnant virtue that's unsatisfying in itself and never impresses others."

These words made me shudder, but I saw clearly that I no longer had the right to oppose them; the criminal co-operation of that immoral woman had become necessary to me, and I had to treat her with consideration. This is one of the fatal disadvantages of vice: as soon as we abandon ourselves to it, it places us in bondage to people whom we would otherwise scorn. And so I accepted all of Madame de Verquin's obligingness. Every night Senneval gave me new proof of his love, and I spend the next six months in such a passionate turmoil that I scarcely had time to think.

My eyes were opened by a disastrous consequence: I became pregnant. I nearly died of despair when I discovered my condition. Madame de Verquin was amused by it. "However," she said, "we must save appearances. Since it wouldn't be very decent for you to have your baby in my house, Senneval's colonel and I have made some arrangements. He's going to give Senneval a leave. You'll go to Metz, he'll join you there a few days later, and then, with his aid, you'll give birth to the illicit fruit of your love. Afterward, you'll both come back here, one after the other, the same as you'll have left."

I had to obey. As I've already said, monsieur, we place ourselves at the mercy of all men and all situations when we've been unfortunate enough to sink into sin; we give rights over ourselves to everyone in the world, we become the slaves of every living being as soon as we forget ourselves to the point of becoming the slaves of our passions.

Everything took place as Madame de Verquin had said. On the third day, Senneval and I were in Metz together, in the house of a midwife whose address I'd been given before I left Nancy, and there I gave birth to a boy. Senneval, who had never stopped showing the most tender and delicate feelings for me, seemed to love me even more as soon as I had doubled his existence, as he put it. He was full of consideration for me; he begged me to leave his son to him, swore that he would take all possible care of him for the rest of his life, and wouldn't think of returning to Nancy until he had fulfilled his obligations to me.

It was not until he was about to leave that I dared to point out to him how unhappy I was going to be because of the sin he had made me commit, and to suggest that we atone for it by consecrating our union before the altar. Senneval, who hadn't expected this, became upset.

"Alas," he said, "it's not within my power. I'm still a minor, so I'd have to have my father's consent. What would our marriage be without it? Besides, I'm by no means a good match for you. As Madame de Verquin's niece" (this was what everyone in Nancy believed) "you can expect something better. Believe me, Florville, the best thing we can do is to forget our mistakes. You can count on my discretion."

These words came as a shock to me, and they made me painfully aware of the enormity of my sin. My pride prevented me from replying, but my grief was all the more bitter. If anything had hidden the horror of my conduct from me, it was, I confess, the hope of making amends for it some day by marrying my lover. What a credulous girl I was ! Although I should no doubt have been enlightened by Madame de Verquin's perversity, I hadn't believed that a man could amuse himself by seducing an unfortunate girl and then abandoning her, that the sentiment of honor, so highly respected among men, could be totally inoperative with regard to us, and that our weakness could justify an insult which one man could not inflict on another without risking his life. I saw that I was both the victim and the dupe of the man for whom I would gladly have given my life. This terrible realization nearly put me into my grave. Senneval didn't leave me; he took care of me the same as before, but he never spoke of my suggestion again, and I had too much pride to mention the cause of my despair to him a second time. He went away as soon as he saw that I'd recovered.

Determined never to go back to Nancy, and realizing that I was seeing my lover for the last time in my life, I felt all my wounds reopening when I said good-by to him. But I had the strength to withstand that final blow . . . How cruel he was ! He left, he tore himself away from my bosom wet with my tears, without shedding a single tear of his own !

Such is the result of the vows of love we're foolish enough to believe ! The more sensitive we are, the more completely our seducers forsake us . . . The traitors ! The degree to which they abandon us is in proportion to our efforts to keep them with us.

Senneval had taken his child and placed him in a country home where it was impossible for me to find him. He wanted to deprive me of the sweet consolation of cherishing and bringing up that tender fruit of our union. It was as though he wanted me to forget everything that might still bind us to each other, and I did, or rather I thought I did.

I decided to leave Metz immediately and not go back to Nancy. I didn't want to quarrel with Madame de Verquin, however. Despite her faults, the fact that she was so closely related to my benefactor was enough to make me treat her with consideration all my life. I wrote to her in the most courteous possible terms, giving my shame over what I'd done in Nancy as my reason for not wanting to return there, and asking her to give me her permission to go back to her brother in Paris. She replied promptly that I was free to do as I pleased, and that I could always count on her friendship. She added that Senneval had not yet returned, that no one knew where he was, and that I was a fool to be so distressed by such trifles.

As soon as I received this letter I went back to Paris and hurried to throw myself at Monsieur de Saint-Prât's feet. My silence and my tears soon informed him of my unhappiness. But I was careful to accuse only myself; I never told him of his sister's deliberate efforts to lead me astray. With his kind, trusting nature, he had never suspected her disorderly life, and believed her to be the most respectable of women. I did nothing to destroy his illusion, and this conduct on my part, which Madame de Verquin knew about, preserved her friendship for me.

Monsieur de Saint-Prât pitied me, made me even more keenly aware of the wrong I'd done, and finally forgave me for it.

"Ah, my child," he said with the gentle gravity of an honorable soul, so different from the odious delirium of crime, "my dear daughter, now you know what it costs to forsake virtue . . . Its practice is so necessary and so intimately bound up with our existence that there's nothing but unhappiness for us as soon as we abandon it. Compare the tranquillity of the state of innocence in which you left this house to the terrible turmoil in which you've returned to it. Do the weak pleasures you savored during your downfall compensate for the torments that now rend your heart? Happiness lies only in virtue, my child, and all the sophisms of its detractors will never bring us a single one of its enjoyments. Ah, Florville, you may be sure that those who deny or oppose those sweet enjoyments do so only out of jealousy, for the barbarous pleasure of making others as guilty and unhappy as themselves. They've blinded themselves and want to blind everyone else; they're mistaken and they want everyone else to be mistaken. But if one could see into the depths of their souls, one would find only sorrow and remorse: all those apostles of crime are full of wretchedness and despair. There's not one of them who, if he were sincere, if he could tell the truth, wouldn't admit that his foul words or his dangerous writings had been guided only by his passions. And who can seriously maintain that the foundations of morality can be shaken without risk? Who would dare to say that doing and desiring well must not necessarily be man's purpose?

And how can someone who does only evil expect to be happy in a society whose most powerful interest is that good should be constantly multiplied? But will not even that apologist of crime shudder when he has uprooted from every heart the only thing from which he can expect his preservation? Who will restrain his servants from ruining him if they have ceased to be virtuous? Who will prevent his wife from dishonoring him if he has convinced her that virtue is useless? Who will hold back the hands of his children if he has dared to wither the seeds of good in their hearts? How will his freedom and his possessions be respected if he has said to the powerful, 'Impunity goes with you, and virtue is only an illusion? No matter what that unhappy man's condition, whether he be a husband or a father, rich or poor, a master or a slave, dangers will spring up on all sides of him, and daggers will be raised above his heart from all directions. If he has dared to destroy in man the only duties which balance his perversity, you may be sure that the poor wretch will perish sooner or later, the victim of his own horrible systems.

"Let us leave religion for the moment and, if you like, let us consider man alone. Who would be stupid enough to think that if he breaks all the laws of society, that society which he has outraged can leave him in peace? Is it not in the interest of man, and the laws, he has made for his safety, always to try to destroy whatever is obstructive or harmful? A certain amount of influence or wealth may give the wicked man a fleeting glow of well-being, but how short its duration will be ! He will soon be recognized, unmasked and made an object of public hatred and contempt. Will he then find the apologists of his conduct? Will his partisans come forward to console him? None of them will acknowledge him. Now that he no longer has everything to offer them, they will all cast him off like a burden. Misfortune will surround him, he will languish in disgrace and sorrow, and, no longer having even his own heart as a refuge, he will soon die in despair."

"What, then, is this absurd reasoning of our adversaries? What is this impotent effort to diminish virtue, to dare to say that anything which is not universal is illusory, and that since virtues are only local, none of them can have any reality? What ! Is there no virtue because each person has had to make its own? If different climates and different kinds of temperament have made different kinds of restraints necessary, if, in a word, virtue has multiplied in a thousand forms, does this mean that there is no virtue on earth? One might as well doubt the reality of a river because it splits off into a thousand different streams. What better proof of the existence and necessity of virtue is there than man's need to adapt it to all his different moral codes and to make it the basis of all of them?

"If anyone can find me a single people which lives without virtue, a single one for which benevolence and kindness are not fundamental bonds . . . I will go further: If anyone can show me even an association of criminals which is not held together by a few principles of virtue, then I will abandon its cause. But if, on the contrary, it can be demonstrated to be useful everywhere, if there is no nation, class, group or individual that can do without it, if no man, in short, can live either happily or safely without it, then, my child, am I wrong to urge you never to depart from it?

"You see where your first lapse has led you, Florville ! " continued my benefactor, clasping me in his arms. "If error should solicit you again, if seduction on your weakness should set new traps for you, remember the misery of this first lapse, think of the man who loves you as though you were his own daughter and whose heart is torn by your failings, and you will find in these reflections all the strength required by devotion to virtue, which I want to instill in you forever."

In accordance with these same principles, Monsieur de Saint-Prât didn't offer to let me stay in his house, but he suggested that I go and live with one of his relatives, a woman as famous for the lofty piety of her life as Madame de Verquin was for her immorality. This arrangement pleased me greatly, Madame de Lérince accepted me gladly, and I was installed in her house less than a week after my return to Paris.

Ah, monsieur, what a difference between that respectable woman and the woman I had just left ! If vice and depravity had established their dominion in Madame de Verquin, it was as though Madame de Lérince's heart had become the sanctuary of all the virtues. I had been frightened by Madame de Verquin's depravity; I was consoled by Madame de Lérince's edifying principles. I had found only bitterness and remorse in listening to Madame de Verquin; I found only sweetness and consolations in abandoning myself to Madame de Lérince . . . Ah, monsieur, let me describe that adorable woman whom I shall always love ! It's a tribute that my heart owes to her virtues, and it's impossible for me to resist it.

Madame de Lérince was about forty years old; she still had the bloom of youth, and her air of candor and modesty did much more to make her face beautiful than the divine proportions that nature had given to her features. Some of those who knew her thought that a little too much nobility and majesty made her rather awesome at first sight, but what might have been taken for pride became softened as soon as she spoke. She had such a pure and beautiful soul, such perfect graciousness and such complete frankness that, in spite of oneself, one always became aware of tender feelings gradually arising beside the veneration she inspired at first.

There was nothing exaggerated or superstitious in Madame de Lérince's religion. The principles of her faith resided in an extreme sensibility. The idea of the existence of God, the worship owed to that Supreme Being: such were the keenest enjoyments of that loving soul. She avowed openly that she would be the most wretched of creatures if some sort of perfidious enlightenment should ever force her mind to destroy in her the respect and love she had for her religion.

Still more strongly attached, if possible, to the sublime morality of her religion that to its practices and ceremonies, she made that excellent morality the rule of all her actions. Slander never soiled her lips; she would not tolerate even a jest which might hurt someone's feelings. Full of affection and compassion for others, finding them interesting even in their faults, she was solely concerned with either carefully hiding those faults or gently admonishing them. If others were unhappy, nothing was as gratifying to her as relieving their unhappiness. She didn't wait for the poor to come and implore her aid; she sought them out, she sensed their distress before they expressed it, and joy could be seen shining from her face when she had consoled a widow or provided for an orphan, when she had brought prosperity to a poor family, or when her hands had broken the chains of adversity. And there was nothing harsh or austere with all this: if the pleasures proposed to her were pure, she indulged in them with delight. She even invented pleasures herself, for fear others might be bored in her company.

Wise and enlightened with the moralist, profound with the theologian, she inspired the novelist and smiled on the poet, she astonished the legislator and the statesman, and directed the games of a child. She had every kind of intelligence, but the kind that shone most brightly in her was recognized chiefly by her special care and charming attention in bringing out the intelligence of others or expressing appreciation of it. Living in retirement by inclination, cultivating her friends for their own sake, Madame de Lérince, who could have served as a model for either sex, made all those around her enjoy the peaceful happiness and heavenly delight which is promised to the honest man by the holy god whose image she was.

I won't bore you, monsieur, with the monotonous details of my life during the seventeen years I was fortunate enough to live with that adorable woman. Discussion of morality and piety, as many benevolent acts as it was possible for us to perform: such were the duties that filled our days.

"People are frightened away from religion, my dear Florville," Madame de Lérince once said to me, "only because awkward guides point out nothing but its restraints to them, without offering them its sweetness. Can there be a man absurd enough to open his eyes to the universe and still dare not to agree that such wonders could only be the work of an all-powerful God? Once this first truth has been realized --- and does one require anything more than one's heart in order to become convinced of it? -- how can anyone be so cruel and barbarous as to refuse his homage to the benevolent God who created him?

"But the diversity of religions is cited as an objection: their falsity is thought to be proved by their multitude. What sophistry ! Is not the existence of a supreme God proved more irrefutably by this unanimity of all peoples in recognizing and serving a God, and by this tacit avowal imprinted in the hearts of all men, than by the sublimities of nature? What ! Man cannot live without adopting a God, he cannot question himself without finding evidence of Him within himself, he cannot open his eyes without seeing traces of Him everywhere, and yet he dares to doubt His existence !

"No, Florville, there are no atheists in good faith. Pride, stubbornest, the passions: those are the destructive weapons of that god who constantly revivifies Himself in man's heart or reason. And when each beat of that heart and each bright ray of that reason offer me that incontestable Being, shall I refuse my homage to Him? Shall I rob Him of the tribute which His goodness allows my weakness? Shall I not humiliate myself before His greatness, and ask Him to help me endure the miseries of life and participate in His glory some day? Shall I not aspire to the favor of spending eternity in His bosom, or shall I risk spending that eternity in a frightful abyss of torments because I've refused to accept the indubitable proofs of that great Being's existence which He has been kind enough to give me? My child, does that appalling choice permit even a moment's reflection? Ah, you who stubbornly refuse to let yourselves recognize the letters of fire that God has traced in the depths of your hearts, be just for at least a moment, and, if only out of pity for yourselves, yield to this invincible argument of Pascal's: 'If there is no God, what does it matter to you if you believe in Him, what harm does it do you? And if there is a god, what risks will you be taking if you refuse Him your faith?'

"But you say, skeptics, that you don't know what tribute to pay to this God; you're repelled by the multitude of religions. Very well, examine them all, I have no objections; then afterward come and tell me sincerely in which one of them you find the most grandeur and majesty. Deny if you can, Christians, that the religion in which you were fortunate enough to be born is the one where characteristics appear to you the holiest and most sublime; seek elsewhere such great mysteries, such pure dogmas, such consoling morality; find in another religion the ineffable sacrifice of a God in favor of His creature, see in it more beautiful promises, a more appealing future, a greater and more sublime God ! No, you cannot, philosopher of the day; you cannot, slave of your pleasures whose faith changes with the physical state of your nerves, so that you are impious in the fire of the passions and a believer as soon as they are calmed; you cannot, I tell you. Sentiment constantly acknowledges the God your mind combats. He always exists beside you, even in the midst of your errors. Break the chains which bind you to crime and that holy and majestic God will never leave the temple He has built in your heart.

"It is in the depths of the heart, my dear Florville, even more than in the mind, that we must seek the necessity of that god whom everything indicates and proves to us. It is also from the heart that we must receive the necessity of the worship we devote to Him. And it is the heart alone, my dear friend, that will soon convince you that the noblest and purest of all religions is the one in which we were born. Let us therefore practice that sweet and consoling religion with exactitude and joy. May it fill our most beautiful moments in this world, may we cherish it until we are gradually led to the end of our life, and may it be by a path of love and delights that we go to place in the bosom of God that soul which emanated from Him, which was formed solely to know Him, and which we should have enjoyed only to believe in Him, and which we should have enjoyed only to believe in Him and worship Him."

That's how Madame de Lérince spoke to me, that's how my mind was strengthened by her advice, and how my soul was refined beneath her holy wing. But, as I've told you, I'm going to pass in silence over the little details of my life in that house and dwell only on what's essential. It's my sins that I must reveal to you, generous and sensitive man, and when heaven has allowed me to live peacefully in the path of virtue, I have only to be thankful and remain silent.

I continue to write to Madame de Verquin. I heard from her regularly twice a month. I should no doubt have stopped writing to her, and I was more or less obliged to do so by my better principles and the reformation of my life, but what I owed to Monsieur de Saint-Prât, the hope of perhaps receiving news of my son some day, and, most of all, I must confess, a secret feeling which still drew me toward the place to which cherished people had bound me in the past -- all these things made me inclined to continue our correspondence, which she was courteous enough to maintain regularly. I tried to convert her, I praised the sweetness of the life I was leading, but she called it an illusion. She never stopped making fun of my resolutions or combating them, and, still firm in her own, she assured me that nothing in the world could weaken them. She told me of the new girls she had converted to her principles for her own amusement, and she claimed that their docility was much greater than mine. Their multiple lapses from virtue, said that perverse woman, were little triumphs which she was always delighted to win, and the pleasure of leading those young hearts into evil consoled her for not being able to do as much of it as her imagination dictated to her.

I often asked Madame de Lérince to lend me her eloquent pen in order to overthrow my adversary, and she was glad to do so. Madame de Verquin replied to us; her sophisms, sometimes very powerful, forced us to resort to the more victorious arguments of a sensitive soul, in which was inevitably found, Madame de Lérince rightly claimed, everything that could destroy vice and confound unbelief.

I occasionally asked Madame de Verquin for news of the man I still loved, but she was always either unwilling or unable to give me any.

The time has come, monsieur; I must tell you of the second catastrophe of my life, the cruel event that breaks my heart each time it presents itself to my imagination. When you have heard it and learned from it the horrible crime of which I am guilty, you will no doubt give up the flattering plans you made with regard to me.

Although Madame de Lérince's house was as orderly as I've described it to you, she nevertheless opened it to a few friends. One day Madame de Dulfort, a middle-aged lady who had once belonged to the household of the Princess of Piedmont, and who came to see us very often asked Madame de Lérince for permission to introduce to her a young man who had been expressly recommended to her, and whom she would be glad to bring into a house where the examples of virtue he would constantly receive could not fail to contribute to forming his heart. My protectress apologized at first, saying that she never received young men; then, vanquished by her friend's earnest entreaties, she consented to see the Chevalier de Saint-Ange.

He appeared. Whether from a presentiment or any other reason you may care to name, monsieur, as soon as I saw that young man I began to quiver all over without being able to determine the cause. I was on the verge of fainting. . . . Not seeking the reason for that strange reaction, I attributed it to some inner indisposition, and Saint-Ange stopped troubling me.

But while he had agitated me at first sight, a similar reaction had also taken place in him, as he later told me himself. He was filled with great veneration for the house into which he had been admitted that he didn't dare to forget himself to the point of revealing the flame that was consuming him. And so three months went by before he ventured to say anything about it to me; but his eyes expressed his feelings so vividly that it was impossible for me to mistake their meaning. Determined not to relapse into a sin which had caused the greatest unhappiness of my life, and strengthened now by better principles, I was ready a score of times to inform Madame de Lérince of the feelings I thought I discerned in Saint-Ange; but at the last moment I was always held back by the alarm I was afraid of causing her, and so I said nothing. This was undoubtedly the wrong decision, for it was the cause of the frightful disaster I will soon relate to you.

We were in the habit of spending six months of every year in Madame de Lérince's attractive country house five miles outside of Paris. Monsieur de Saint-Prât often came to see us there. Unfortunately for me, he had an attack of gout that year and was unable to come. I say "unfortunately for me," monsieur, because, having naturally more confidence in him that in Madame de Lérince, I would have told him things I was never able to bring myself to tell anyone else, and telling them to him would no doubt have prevented the deadly accident that happened.

Saint-Ange asked Madame de Lérince for permission to come with us, and since Madame de Dulfort also requested this favor for him, it was granted.

Everyone in our group was rather uneasy about our lack of knowledge of this young man; nothing very clear or definite was known about his life. Madame de Dulfort had told us he was the son of a provincial gentleman to whom she was related. As for Saint-Ange himself, he sometimes forgot what Madame de Dulfort had said and referred to himself as Piedmontese, a claim which seemed rather well supported by the way he spoke Italian. Although he was old enough to something in life, he hadn't yet embarked on any career and showed no inclination to do so. He had a very handsome face, worthy of an artist's brush. His manners were excellent, he always spoke courteously, and he gave every indication of being well bred; but through all this there was a prodigious intensity, a kind of impetuosity in his character which sometimes frightened us.

The curb he had tried to impose on his feelings had only made them grow. As soon as he was in Madame de Lérince's country house it became impossible for him to conceal from me. I trembled . . . but I summoned up enough self-control to show him only pity.

"Really, monsieur," I said to him, "you must have a false idea of your own worth, or else you have time to waste, since you spend it with a woman twice your age. But even assuming that I should be foolish enough to listen to you, what ridiculous aims would you dare to form concerning me?"

"My only aim would be to bind myself to you by the holiest of ties, mademoiselle. How little respect you would have for me if you thought I had any other ! "

"Let me assure you, monsieur, that I would never offer the public the strange spectacle of a woman of thirty-four marrying a boy of seventeen."

"Ah, cruel woman, would you be aware of that slight difference if your heart contained even a thousandth of the fire that's consuming mine?"

"It's certain, monsieur, that for my part I'm quite calm. I've been calm for many years; and I hope I shall continue for as long as it pleases God to let me languish on this earth."

"You deprive me of even the hope of moving you to pity some day."

"I go further: I dare to forbid you to speak to me of your madness any longer."

"Ah, fair Florville, do you want my life to be miserable?"

"I want it to be peaceful and happy."

"It can be neither without you."

"No, not until you've destroyed the ridiculous feelings you never should have conceived. Try to overcome them, try to control yourself, and your tranquility will return."

"I can't."

"You don't want to. We must part before you can succeed. If you spend two years without seeing me, your agitation will pass, you'll forget me, and you'll be happy."

"Ah, never ! Never shall I find happiness anywhere but at your feet. . . ."

Just then the others rejoined us, so our first conversation stopped at that point.

Three days later, Saint-Ange succeeded in being alone with me again and tried to resume our discussion in the same tone as before. This time I imposed silence on him so sternly that his tears flowed abundantly. He left me abruptly, after telling me that I was driving him to despair and that he would soon take his own life if I continued to treat him as I was doing. Then he turned around, hurried back to me like a madman and said, "Mademoiselle, you don't know the soul you're insulting ! No, you don't know it. . . . Let me tell you that I'm capable of going to violent extremes . . . extremes that you may be far from thinking of . . . Yes, I'll resort to them a thousand times rather than renounce the happiness of belonging to you." And he left in terrible grief.

I was never more strongly tempted to speak to Madame de Lérince than I was then, but, as I've already said, I was restrained by the fear of harming Saint-Ange. I said nothing. For a week he fled from me, scarcely speaking to me, avoiding me at table, in the drawing room, and during our walks. All this was no doubt done in order to see whether his change of conduct would make an impression on me. It would have been an effective means if I had shared his feelings, but I was so far from doing so that I hardly seemed to be aware of his maneuvers.

Finally he came up to me in the garden and said, in the most violent state imaginable, "Mademoiselle, I've at last succeed in calming myself. Your advice has had the effect on me that you expected: you can see how tranquil I've become. I've tried to find you alone only because I want to tell you good-by . . . Yes, I'm going away from you forever, mademoiselle, I'm going away . . . You'll never again see the man you hate . . . Oh, no, you'll never see him again ! "

"I'm glad to hear of your plan, monsieur. I like to think that you've become reasonable at last. But," I added smiling, "your conversion doesn't seem very real to me."

"Well, then, how should I be, mademoiselle, in order to convince you of my indifference?"

"Quite different from the way I see you now."

"But at least when I'm gone, when you no longer have the pain of seeing me, perhaps you'll believe that all your efforts have finally succeeded in making me reasonable."

"It's true that only your departure would convince me of it, and I'll continue to advise you to leave."

"Then I must be terribly repulsive to you ! "

"You're a charming man, monsieur, who ought to pursue conquests of a different value and leave me in peace, because it's impossible for me to listen to you."

"But you will listen to me ! " he said furiously. "Yes, cruel woman, you'll listen, no matter what you say, to the feelings of my fiery soul, and to the assurance that there's nothing in the world I won't do either to deserve you or to obtain you . . . And don't believe in my pretended departure," he went on impetuously. "I told you about it only to test you . . . Do you really think I'd leave you? Do you think I could tear myself away from the place where you are? I'd rather die a thousand deaths ! Hate me, traitress, hate me, since that's my unhappy fate, but never hope to overcome the love for you with which I'm burning . . . "

When he spoke these last words he was in such a state that, by a mischance which I've never been able to understand, I was deeply moved and turned away from him to hide my tears. I left him in the thicket where he had joined me. He didn't follow me. I heard him throw himself on the ground and abandon himself to the excess of a horrible delirium . . . and I must admit to you, monsieur, that although I was quite certain of having no feeling of love for him, whether from commiseration or memory it was impossible for me not to give vent to my own emotion.

"Alas," I said to myself, yielding to my sorrow, "Senneval spoke to me in the same way ! It was in the same terms that he expressed his passion to me . . . And also in a garden, a garden like this one . . . He told me he would always love me, and yet he cruelly deceived me ! Good heavens, he was the same age ! . . . Ah, Senneval, Senneval, are you trying to take away my peace of mind again? Have you reappeared in this seductive guise to drag me into the abyss a second time? Away, coward, away ! I now abhor even your memory ! "

I wiped my eyes and stayed in my room till supper time. I then went downstairs. But Saint-Ange didn't appear, having announced that he was ill. And the next day he was adroit enough to let me see only serenity on his face. I was deceived by him: I really believed he had exercised enough self-control to overcome his passion. I was mistaken, the treacherous deceiver ! . . . Alas, what am I saying, monsieur? I no longer owe him invectives . . . I owe him only my tears and my remorse.

He appeared so calm only because he had already made his plans. Two days went by like this, and toward the evening of the third he publicly announced his departure. He made arrangements with Madame de Dulfort, his protectress, concerning their common affairs in Paris.

We all went to bed . . . Forgive me, monsieur, for the agitation which the story of that terrible catastrophe arouses in me in advance; it never presents itself to my memory without making me shudder with horror.

Since it was a very hot night, I lay down on my bed almost naked. As soon as my maid left, I put out my candle. A sewing bag had unfortunately remained open on my bed, because I'd just cut some gauze I was going to need the next day. My eyes had scarcely begun to close when I heard a sound . . . I quickly sat up. I felt a hand seize me . . .

"This time you won't get away from me, Florville," said Saint-Ange, for it was he. "Forgive the excessiveness of my passion, but don't try to escape from it. I must make you mine ! "

"Infamous seducer ! " I cried. "Get out immediately, or fear the effects of my anger ! "

"I fear nothing except not being able to possess you cruel girl ! " said that ardent young man, throwing himself on me so skillfully and in such a state of frenzy that I became his victim before I was able to do anything to prevent it . . .

Enraged by his audacity and determined to do anything rather than submit to it any further, I broke away from his and snatched up the scissors that were lying at my feet. But even in my fury I retained a certain amount of self-control: I sought his arm, intending to stab him in it, much more to frighten him by my resolution than to punish him as he deserved. When he felt my movements he redoubled the violence of his own.

"Traitor ! " I cried, stabbing what I thought was his arm, "Get out this instant ! And blush with shame for your crime ! "

Oh monsieur, a fatal hand had guided mine! The poor young man uttered a cry and fell to the floor. I quickly lit a candle and bent over him . . . Good heavens! I had stabbed him in the heart! He died . . . I threw myself onto his bleeding body and feverishly clasped it to my agitated bosom . . . I pressed my mouth to his, trying to bring back his departed soul. I washed his wound with my tears . . .

"Ah, you whose only crime was to love me too much," I said in the frenzy of despair, "did you deserve such a death? Should you have died by the hand of the woman for whom you would have sacrificed your life? Unhappy young man, image of him whom I once adored, if all I must do is to love you in order to bring you back to life, let me tell you at this cruel moment when you can unfortunately no longer hear me, let me tell you, if your soul is still palpitating, that I wish I could revive you at the cost of my own life . . . I want you to know that I was never indifferent to you, that I never saw you without emotion, and that my feelings for you were perhaps far superior to the weak love that burned in your heart."

With these words I fell unconscious onto the body of that unfortunate young man. My maid came in, having heard the sound of my fall. She brought me back to my senses, then she joined me in trying to revive Saint-Ange. Alas, all our efforts were in vain. We left that fateful room, carefully locked its door, took the key with us and immediately hurried to Monsieur de Saint-Prât's house in Paris. I had him awakened, gave him the key to that sinister chamber and told him my horrible story. He pitied me and consoled me, and then, even though he was ill, he went straight to Madame de Lérince's house. Since it was quite close to Paris, he arrived as everyone was getting up, before the events of the night had become known. Never have friends or relatives conducted themselves better. Far from imitating those stupid or ferocious people whose only concern in such crises is to make known everything that can bring dishonor or unhappiness to themselves and those around them, they acted in such a way that even the servants scarcely had any suspicion of what had occurred.

At this point, Mademoiselle de Florville broke off her narrative because of the tears that were choking her; then she said to Monsieur de Courval, "Well, monsieur now will you marry a woman capable of such a murder? Will you hold in your arms a creature who deserves the full severity of the law, a wretched creature who is constantly tormented by her crime, and who has never had a peaceful night since that cruel moment? No monsieur, there has never been a single night when my unfortunate victim hasn't presented himself to me covered with the blood I tore from his heart ! "

"Be calm, mademoiselle, be calm, I beg you," said Monsieur de Courval, mingling his tears with hers. "With the sensitive soul you've been given by nature, I understand your remorse. But there's not even the shadow of a crime in that fatal event. It was a terrible misfortune, of course, but that's all. There was nothing premeditated in it, nothing heinous; your only desire was to ward off an odious attack . . . In short, it was a murder committed by chance, in self-defense. Put your mind at rest, mademoiselle, I insist on it . . . The sternest tribunal would do nothing except wipe your tears. Ah, how mistaken you were if you were afraid that such an event would make you lose the rights to my heart which your personal qualities have given you. No, no, fair Florville, far from dishonoring you, it enhances your virtues in my eyes, and only makes you worthier of a consoling hand that will make you forget your sorrows."

"Monsieur de Saint-Prât also said what you've been kind enough to tell me," said Mademoiselle de Florville, "but the reproaches of my conscience can't be stifled by the great kindness you've both shown me, and nothing will ever soothe its remorse. But it doesn't matter; let me go on, monsieur, because you must be apprehensive about the outcome of all this."

And Mademoiselle de Florville continued her story:

Madame de Dulfort was grief-stricken; aside from Saint-Ange's intrinsic attractiveness he had been so specially recommended to her that she couldn't fail to lament his loss. But she saw the reasons for silence, she realized that a public scandal would only ruin me without bringing her protégé back to life, and she said nothing. Madame de Lérince, despite the severity of her principles and the extreme propriety of her morals, behaved still better, if that's possible, because prudence and humanity are the distinctive characteristics of true piety. She began by telling her household that I had capriciously decided to go back to Paris during the night in order to enjoy the cool weather, that she had been informed of this whim on my part, and that she had no objection to it because she herself was planning to go to Paris that evening for supper. On this pretext, she sent all her servants there. As soon as she was alone with Monsieur de Saint-Prât and Madame de Dulfort, she sent for the parish priest. Madame de Lérince's pastor was as wise and enlightened as herself; he gave Madame de Dulfort an official attestation without raising any objections, and then, with two of his servants, he secretly buried the unfortunate victim of my fury.

When these precautions had been taken, everyone reappeared and took an oath of secrecy. Monsieur de Saint-Prât came to calm me by telling me about everything that had been done to make sure that my act would remain shrouded in oblivion. He seemed to want me to resume my life in Madame de Lérince's house as before. She was ready to receive me. I told him I couldn't bring myself to do it. He then advised me to seek diversion. Madame de Verquin, with whom I'd never ceased to be in correspondence, as I've already told you, monsieur, was still urging me to come and spend a few months with her. I discussed this idea with her brother, he approved of it, and a week later I went to Lorraine. But the memory of my crime pursued me everywhere and nothing was able to calm me.

I often awoke in the middle of the night, thinking I could still hear poor Saint-Ange's moans and cries; I saw him bleeding at my feet, reproaching me for my barbarity, assuring me that the memory of my horrible act would hound me to the end of my days, and that I didn't know the heart I'd pierced.

One night I dreamed that Senneval - that wretched lover whom I hadn't forgotten, since he alone still drew me toward Nancy - showed me two corpses: that of Saint-Ange and that of a woman who was unknown to me. He shed tears on both of them, and pointed to a nearby coffin bristling with thorns, which seemed to have been opened for me. I awoke in a state of terrible agitation; a multitude of confused feelings arose in my soul, and a secret voice seemed to say to me, "Yes, as long as you live, your poor victim will draw tears of blood from you which will become more agonizing every day and the goad of your remorse will constantly grow sharper, rather than duller."

Such was the state in which I reached Nancy, monsieur. A thousand new sorrows were awaiting me there; once the hand of fate descends upon us, its blows increase until they crush us.

I went to visit Madame de Verquin; she had asked me to come in her last letter, and she had said that she was looking forward to seeing me, but little did I realize the conditions under which we were going to share the joy of seeing each other again. She was on her deathbed when I arrived. Merciful heaven, who would have thought it! She had written to me only two weeks before, telling me of her present pleasures and announcing others to come. Such are the plans of mortals: it's while they're forming them, in the midst of their amusements, that merciless death comes to cut the thread of their days; living without ever concerning themselves with that fateful moment, as though they were going to be on earth forever, they vanish into the dark cloud of immortality, uncertain of the fate that lies in store for them.

Allow me, monsieur, to interrupt the story of my adventures a few moments to tell you about Madame de Verquin's death, and to describe to you the frightening stoicism which accompanied her to the grave.

After an escapade that was foolish for her age (she was then fifty-two), Madame de Verquin had jumped into the water to cool herself. She fainted and was brought home in an alarming state. Pneumonia set in the following day, and on the sixth day she was told that she had no more than twenty-four hours to live. This news didn't frighten her; she knew I was going to come, and she ordered that I be received.

I arrived on the very evening when, according to her doctor, she was going to die. She'd had herself placed in a room furnished with the greatest possible taste and elegance. She was lying, casually dressed, on a voluptuous bed whose lilac-colored silk curtains were pleasantly set off by garlands of natural flowers. Every corner was adorned by bouquets of carnations, jasmine, tuberoses and roses; she was pulling off the petals of some of them, and she'd already covered her bed and the whole room with them. She held out her hand to me as soon as she saw me.

"Come, Florville," she said, "embrace me on my bed of flowers . . . How tall and beautiful you've become ! Ah, yes, my child, virtue has done you good . . . You've been told about my condition . . . You've been told about it, Florville . . . I know about it too . . . In a few hours I'll be gone; I'd never have thought I'd have so little time to spend with you when I saw you again . . . "

She saw my eyes fill with tears. "Come, come, foolish girl," she said, "don't be childish . . . Do you really think there's any reason to feel sorry for me? Haven't I had as much pleasure as any other woman in the world? I'm losing all the years when I'd have had to give up my pleasures, and what would I have done without them? The truth is that I don't pity myself at all for not living to be older than I am now. Before long, no man would have wanted me, and I've never had any desire to live to an age when I'd arouse repugnance. Only believers have any reason to fear death, my child; always between heaven and hell, not knowing which will open to receive them, they're torn by anxiety. As for me, I hope for nothing, and I'm sure of being no more unhappy after my death than I was before my life. I'm going to sleep peacefully in the bosom of nature, without regret or grief, without remorse or apprehension. I've asked to be buried in my bower of jasmine; my place is already being prepared in it. I'll be there, Florville, and the atoms that come from my disintegrating body will nourish the flowers I've loved most of all. And next year," she went on, stroking my cheek with a bouquet of those flowers, "when you smell them you'll be inhaling your dead friend's soul; the fragrance will force its way into the fibers of your brain, give you pleasant ideas and make you think of me."

My tears began to flow again. I clasped the hands of that unfortunate woman and tried to make her exchange her frightful materialistic ideas for a less impious viewpoint, but as soon as she became aware of my intention she pushed me away in alarm.

"Oh, Florville," she cried, "please don't poison my last moments with your errors ! Let me die in peace. I hated those errors all my life, and I'm not going to adopt them now that I'm about to die."

I said nothing. What could my feeble eloquence have done against such firmness? I would only have distressed her without converting her; simple human kindness opposed it. She pulled her bell cord and I immediately heard sweet, melodious music which seemed to be coming from an adjoining room.

"This is how I intend to die, Florville," said that Epicurean. "Isn't it better than being surrounded by priests who would fill my last moments with turmoil, alarm and despair? No, I want to teach your pious believers that it's possible to die in peace without being like them. I want to convince them that it doesn't require religion, but only courage and reason."

Time was passing. A notary came in; she had sent for him. The music stopped. She dictated a few last wishes. She had no children and she had been a widow for a number of years, so she was able to dispose of many things as she saw fit; she left legacies to her friends and her servants. Then she took a little coffer from a writing desk near her bed.

"Here's all I have left now," she said, "a little cash and a few jewels. Let's amuse ourselves the rest of the evening. There are six of you in my room now; I'm going to divide all this into six parts and we'll have a lottery. Each one of you will keep whatever he wins."

I was amazed by her composure. It seemed incredible to me that she could have so many things with which to reproach herself, and yet approach her last moment with such calm - a pernicious effect of unbelief. If the horrible deaths of some wicked people make us shudder, how much more frightened we ought to be by such steadfast impenitence !

What she wanted was done. She had a magnificent meal served. She ate from several dishes and drank liqueurs and Spanish wines, for the doctor had told her that in her condition it didn't matter.

The lots were drawn and each of us received nearly two thousand francs in gold or jewels. This little game was scarcely over when she was seized with a violent attack.

"Well, is this it?" She asked the doctor, still with complete serenity.

"I'm afraid so, madame."

"Then come, Florville," she said, holding out her arms to me, "come and receive my last farewells. I want to die on the bosom of virtue . . . "

She clasped me tightly in her arms and her beautiful eyes closed forever.

Being a stranger in that house and no longer having any reason to stay there, I left immediately. I leave you to imagine the state I was in, and how much that spectacle still darkened my mind.

The gap between Madame de Verquin's way of thinking and mine was too great to allow me to love her with complete sincerity. Furthermore, she was the first cause of my dishonor and all the calamities that had followed it. And yet that woman, sister of the only man who had really taken care of me, had never treated me with anything but kindness and had continued to do so even on her deathbed. My tears were therefore quite sincere, and their bitterness redoubled when I reflected that, with her excellent qualities, that miserable creature had involuntarily brought on her own perdition, and that, already cast out from God's bosom, she was no doubt painfully undergoing the punishment she had earned by her depraved life. However, the thought of god's supreme goodness came to soothe the distress that these ideas had caused in me. I fell to my knees and dared to pray the almighty to forgive that unfortunate soul; even though I myself had great need of heaven's mercy, I dared to implore it for someone else. To sway heaven as much as was in my power, I added two hundred francs of my own money to what I had won in Madame de Verquin's lottery and had it all distributed among the poor of her parish.

Her last wishes were scrupulously respected; she had made her arrangements so well that they could not fail to be carried out. She was buried in her bower of jasmine. At her head was a black marble obelisk on which this single word was carved: Vixit

Thus died the sister of my dearest friend. Full of intelligence and knowledge, richly endowed with charms and talents, Madame de Verquin could have deserved, if she had behaved differently, the love and esteem of all those who knew her; instead, she obtained only their contempt. Her licentiousness had increased as she grew older. Someone who has no principles is never more dangerous than at the age when he has ceased to blush: depravity corrupts his heart, he refines his first failings, and gradually he begins to commit crimes, thinking he is still only indulging in follies. But I was constantly surprised by the incredible blindness of Madame de Verquin's brother. Such is the distinctive mark of candor and goodness; virtuous people, never suspecting the evil of which they themselves are incapable, are readily taken in by the first scoundrel who seizes upon them, and that's why there's so much ease and so little glory in deceiving them. The insolent rogue who does it is only working to demean himself, and without even proving his talent for vice, he only lends greater brilliance to virtue.

In losing Madame de Verquin, I'd also lost all hope of learning anything about my lover and my son; as you can well imagine, I hadn't dared to question her about them when I saw the terrible state she was in.

Crushed by this catastrophe and exhausted from a journey made in a painful state of mind, I decided to rest for a time in Nancy, at the inn where I already had a room, without seeing anyone at all, since Monsieur de Saint-Prât had seemed to want me to conceal my name. It was there that I wrote to my dear protector, having resolved not to leave until I'd received his answer:

A wretched girl who is nothing to you, monsieur, and who can lay claim only to your pity, endlessly troubles your life; instead of speaking to you only of the grief you must be feeling over the loss you have just suffered, she dares to speak to you of herself, to ask you for your orders and to await them . . .

But it was ordained that misfortune was to follow me everywhere, and that I was to be constantly either a witness or a victim of its sinister effects.

One evening I came back to the inn rather late after having gone out for a breath of fresh air with my maid and a footman whom I had hired temporarily on arriving in Nancy. Everyone else had already gone to bed. As I was about to go into my room, a woman in her early fifties, tall and still beautiful, whom I'd known by sight since my arrival at the inn, suddenly came out of her room, next to mine, and, armed with a dagger, rushed into a room across the hall. My natural inclination was to see . . . I hurried forward followed by my servants, and in the twinkling of an eye, before we had time to stop her or even call out to her, we saw that wretched woman throw herself on another woman, stab her in the heart a dozen times, then go back to her room in a frenzied state, without having seen us. We thought at first that she'd gone mad; we couldn't understand her crime, for which no motive was apparent to us. When I saw that my maid and my footman were about to cry out, an overpowering impulse, whose cause was unknown to me, made me order them to remain silent, seize them by the arm, pull them into my room and close the door behind us.

We soon heard a frightful commotion: the woman who had just been stabbed had managed to stagger to the head of the stairs, screaming horribly. Before she died she was able to name her murderer. Since it was known that we were the last to enter the inn, we were arrested at the same time as the murder. However, since the victim's accusation had cast no suspicions on us, we were merely ordered not to leave the inn until the end of the trial.

The murderer was imprisoned, but she admitted nothing and firmly maintained that she was innocent. My servants and I were the only witnesses. We were summoned to testify. I had to speak, and I also had to conceal the agitation that was secretly devouring me. I deserved death as much as the woman my forced testimony was going to send to the scaffold, for although the circumstances had been different, I was guilty of the same crime. I would have given anything to avoid that cruel testimony. It seemed to me as I spoke that with each word a drop of blood was torn from my heart. But our statements had to be complete; we reported everything we had seen.

We later learned that no matter how firmly convinced the authorities may have been that the crime was committed by that woman, whose motive had been to do away with a rival, it would have been impossible to convict her if it hadn't been for us, because a man involved in the situation had fled and might have been suspected; but the poor woman's doom was sealed by our testimony - especially that of my footman, who happened to be attached to the inn where the crime had been committed - which we could not have refused to give without placing ourselves in danger.

The last time I confronted her, she examined me with great astonishment and asked me how old I was.

"I'm thirty-four," I replied.

"Thirty-four? . . . And you're from this province?"

"No, madame."

"Your name is Florville?"

"Yes, that's what I'm called."

"I don't know you," she said, "but you're an honest woman, and you're said to be respected in this town; unfortunately that's enough for me . . . Mademoiselle," she went on with agitation, "I had a dream in which you appeared to me in the midst of the horrors that now surround me. You were there with my son . . . Yes, I'm a mother, and an unhappy one, as you can see. You had the same face, the same figure, the same dress . . . And the scaffold was before my eyes . . . "

"A dream," I exclaimed, "a dream, madame ! " I immediately recalled my own dream, and I was struck by her features: I recognized her as the woman who had appeared to me with Senneval, near the coffin bristling with thorns. Tears welled up in my eyes. The more I examined that woman, the more I was tempted to retract my testimony. I wanted to ask to be executed in her stead, I wanted to flee and yet I couldn't tear myself away . . .

Having no reason to doubt my innocence, the officials merely separated us when they saw the terrible state in which she'd placed me. I went back to my inn in despair, overwhelmed by a multitude of feelings whose cause I couldn't discern. The next day, that miserable woman was put to death.

On that same day I received Monsieur de Saint-Prât's answer. He urged me to come back. Nancy was, of course, no longer very pleasant to me, after the grim scenes it had just offered me, so I left it immediately and set out for Paris, pursued by the new ghost of that woman, who seemed to cry out to me at every moment, "It's you who've sent me to my death, wretched girl, and you don't know who it is that your own hand has pushed into the grave ! "

Crushed by all these afflictions and persecuted by an equal number of sorrows, I asked Monsieur de Saint-Prât to find me a retreat in which I could end my days in the deepest solitude, and in the most rigorous duties of my religion. He suggested the one in which you found me, monsieur. I took up residence in it that same week, and from then on I left it only twice a month, to visit my dear protector and to spend a little time with Madame de Lérince. But heaven, which seems determined to deal me a painful blow every day, didn't let me enjoy my friendship with Madame de Lérince for long: I had the misfortune of losing her last year. Her affection for me required that I stay with her during those cruel moments, and she, too, breathed her last in my arms.

But who would have believed it, monsieur? Her death was less peaceful than Madame de Verquin's. Since Madame de Verquin had never hoped for anything, she wasn't afraid of losing everything. Madame de Lérince seemed to dread seeing the object of her hope disappear. I had noticed no remorse in Madame de Verquin, who should have been overwhelmed by it; Madame de Lérince, who had never given herself any reason for remorse, felt it keenly. At her death, Madame de Verquin regretted only that she hadn't done enough evil; Madame de Lérince died regretting the good she hadn't done. One covered herself with flowers and lamented only the loss of her pleasures, the other wanted to die on a cross of ashes, and was grieved by the memory of the hours she hadn't devoted to virtue.

I was struck by these contrasts. A little laxity stole over my soul. "Why," I said to myself, "isn't virtue rewarded with calm at that time, when it seems to be granted to misconduct?" But then strengthened by a heavenly voice that seemed to thunder from the depths of my heart, I immediately cried out, "Is it for me to fathom God's will? What I see only assures me of one more merit. Madame de Lérince's fear was the solicitude of virtue; Madame de Verquin's cruel indifference was only the last aberration of crime. Ah, if I have a choice in my last moments, may God grant me the favor of frightening me like Madame de Lérince, rather than numbing me like Madame de Verquin ! "

Such is the last of my adventures, monsieur. For the past two years I've been living at the Convent of the Assumption, where my benefactor placed me. Yes, monsieur, I've been living there for two years, and not once have I had a moment of rest, not once have I spent a night without seeing the image of poor Saint-Ange and the unfortunate woman whose execution. I caused in Nancy. Now you know the state in which you found me, and the secret things I had to reveal to you. Wasn't it my duty to inform you of them before yielding to the feelings that had deceived you? Now you can see whether it's possible for me to be worthy of you, and whether a woman whose soul is torn by sorrow could bring any joy to your life. Take my advice, monsieur: stop deluding yourself, let me return to the stern seclusion which is the only kind of existence that befits me. If you were to tear me away from it, you would constantly have before your eyes the frightful spectacle of remorse, grief and misfortune.

By the time she had thus ended her story, Mademoiselle de Florville was in a state of violent agitation. Naturally animated, sensitive and delicate, she could not fail to be deeply affected by such a recital of her tribulation.

Monsieur de Courval did not feel that the later events of her story presented any more valid reasons for changing his plans that the earlier ones had done. He did everything he could to calm the woman he loved.

"Let me say again, mademoiselle," he said to her, "that there are fateful and singular things in what you've just told me, but that I don't see a single one that ought to alarm your conscience or damage your reputation. An affair at the age of sixteen, so be it, but there were many excuses on your side: your age, Madame de Verquin's effort to lead you astray, a young man who was no doubt very charming . . . and whom you've never seen since then, have you, mademoiselle? He added with a touch of anxiety. "And you'll probably never see him again . . . "

"Oh, certainly not ! " said Florville, sensing the reasons for his anxiety.

"Well, then, mademoiselle," he said, "let's conclude our arrangements, I beg you, and let me convince you as soon as possible that there's nothing in your story that could diminish, in the heart of an honest man, either the consideration owed to all your virtues or the homage demanded by all your charms."

She asked for permission to return to Paris again to consult her protector for the last time, and promised that she would raise no further objections. He could not refuse to let her fulfill that virtuous duty. She left, and came back a week later with Saint-Prât. Monsieur de Courval showered courteous attentions on him; he made it abundantly clear to him how greatly flattered he was to be able to marry the girl he was kind enough to protect, and he begged him to go on acknowledging her as his relative. Saint-Prât responded graciously to Courval's attentions and continued to give him extremely advantageous notions concerning Mademoiselle de Florville's character.

At last came the day that Courval had desired so much. The ceremony took place, and when the contract was read he was surprised to learn that, without telling any, Monsieur de Saint-Prât had, in consideration of Florville's marriage, doubled the income of four thousand francs a year which he was already giving her, and bequeathed her a hundred thousand francs to be paid to her after his death.

She shed abundant tears when she saw her protector's new kindnesses to her, and at the bottom of her heart she was glad to be able to offer the man who was good enough to marry her a fortune at least equal to his own.

Cordiality, pure joy and reciprocal assurance of esteem and attachments presided over the celebration of that wedding . . . of that fateful wedding whose torches were secretly extinguished by the Furies.

Monsieur de Saint-Prât spend a week in Courval's country house, along with our bridegroom's friends, but the newlyweds did not return to Paris with them: they decided to stay in the country until the beginning of winter, to give themselves time to put their affairs in order so that they would be able to establish a good household in Paris. Monsieur de Saint-Prât was instructed to find them a pleasing residence near his own, to enable them to see each other more often.

Monsieur and Madame de Courval had already spent nearly three months together in the sweet anticipation of all those agreeable arrangements, and they were already certain of her pregnancy, which they had hastened to announce to the good Monsieur de Saint-Prât, when an unexpected event blighted the well-being of the happy couple and changed the tender roses of wedlock into the mournful cypresses of sorrow.

At this point my pen stops . . . I ought to ask my readers for mercy, beg them to go no further . . . Yes, let them stop immediately if they do not wish to shudder with horror . . . Sad condition of mankind on earth, cruel effect of the capriciousness of fate . . . Why should the unhappy Florville, the most virtuous, charming and sensitive girl in the world, have found herself, through an almost inconceivable series of fateful events the most abominable monster that nature could have created?

One evening that tender, loving wife was sitting beside her husband, reading an incredibly gloomy English novel which was causing a great stir at the time.

"There's someone who's almost as unfortunate as I am," she said, throwing down the book.

"As unfortunate as you?" said Monsieur de Courval, clasping his beloved wife in his arms. "Oh, Florville, I thought I'd made you forget your misfortunes ! I see I was mistaken . . . Did you have to say it to me so harshly?"

But Madame de Courval had become as though insensitive: she did not even utter a word in response to his caresses. With an involuntary movement, she pushed his away in alarm, hurried over to a sofa, lay down on it and burst into tears. It was in vain that the worthy Courval threw himself at the feet of the woman he worshiped and begged her either to calm herself or at least tell him the cause of her sudden despair. She continued to repulse him and turn away from him when he tried to dry her tears, until finally, no longer doubting that a pernicious memory of her former passion had come to inflame her anew, he could not help reproaching her a little on the subject.

For a time she listened to him without answering, then she stood up and said, "No, monsieur, you're mistaken in giving that interpretation to the sorrow that overwhelmed me just now. I'm frightened not by memories, but by forebodings . . . I see myself happy with you, monsieur -- yes, very happy -- and I wasn't born for happiness. It's impossible for me to go like this much longer; my destiny is such that the dawn of happiness is always the lightning which precedes a thunderbolt . . . That's what make me shudder: I'm afraid we weren't destined to live together. Perhaps tomorrow I shall no longer be your wife . . . A secret voice cries out from the depths of my heart that all this happiness is only a shadow which is about to vanish like a flower that springs up and is cut down in a single day. So don't accuse me of being capricious or becoming cold toward you, monsieur: I'm guilty only of excessive sensibility and an unhappy tendency to see everything in its most sinister aspect -- a painful result of my afflictions . . . "

Monsieur de Courval was still at her feet, unsuccessfully trying to calm her by his caresses and his words when suddenly (it was about seven o'clock on an evening in October) a servant was insistently asking to speak to Monsieur de Courval. Florville shuddered. Involuntary tears streamed down her cheeks, her legs became unsteady and she sat down; she tried to speak, but her voice died on her lips.

More concerned with his wife's condition than with what his servant had just told him, Monsieur de Courval curtly ordered him to tell the visitor to wait, then he hurried to Florville's aid. But, afraid of succumbing to the secret emotion that was gripping her, and wishing to hide her feelings from the stranger whose arrival had been announced, she stood up forcefully and said, "It's nothing, monsieur, it's nothing . . . Let the gentleman come in."

The servant left and returned a moment later, followed by a man thirty-seven or thirty-eight years old whose face, though quite attractive, bore the marks of a deeply rooted sorrow.

"Father ! " cried the stranger, throwing himself at Monsieur de Courval's feet. "Will you recognize a wretched man who's been separated from you for twenty-two years, and who's been all too severely punished for his cruel misconduct by the calamities that have constantly overwhelmed him ever since he left you?"

"What ! You're my son? Good heavens ! . . . By what event . . . Ingrate ! What made you remember my existence?"

"My heart . . . that heart which has never stopped loving you, despite its guilt . . . Listen to me, father, I have greater misfortunes than my own to reveal to you; please sit down and hear me. And you, madame," continued young Courval, turning to his father's wife, "please forgive me if, immediately after paying my respects to you for the first time in my life, I'm forced to relate some terrible family catastrophes which it's no longer possible to conceal from my father."

"Speak, monsieur, speak," stammered Madame de Courval, looking at him with haggard eyes, "the language of unhappiness isn't new to me: I've known it ever since my childhood."

Staring at her with a kind of involuntary agitation, the young man said to her, "You've been unhappy, madame? Ah, merciful heaven, can you have been as unhappy as we?"

They sat down. Madame de Courval's state would be difficult to describe. She glanced at the visitor, looked down at the floor, sighed from inner turmoil. Monsieur de Courval was weeping while his son tried to calm him and begged him to lend him his attention. Finally the conversation took a more orderly turn.

"I have so many things to tell you, monsieur," said young Courval, "that you'll have to allow me to omit the details and tell you only the main facts. And I want you and madame to give me your word not to interrupt me until I've finished.

"I left you when I fifteen, monsieur. My first impulse was to go to my mother, whom I was blind enough to prefer to you. She'd been separated from you for many years. I rejoined her in Lyons. Her scandalous life alarmed me so much that I had to flee from her to preserve what remained of the sentiments I owed to her. I went to Strasbourg, where the Normandy regiment was garrisoned . . . "

Madame de Courval started, but controlled herself.

"My colonel took a certain interest in me," young Courval went on. "I attracted his attention and he made me a second lieutenant. The following year, I went with the regiment to Nancy, where I fell in love with Madame de Verquin's young niece. I seduced her, had a son by her, then cruelly abandoned her."

At these words, Madame de Courval quivered and a low moan escaped from her chest, but she continued to be firm.

"That wretched adventure was the cause of all my misfortunes. I placed the poor girl's child in the home of a woman who lived near Metz, and who promised to take care of him. A short time later I returned to my regiment. My conduct was strongly condemned. Since the young lady hadn't been able to reappear in Nancy, I was accused of having ruined her. Too charming not to have interested the whole town, she found avengers there. I fought a duel, killed my adversary and went to Turin with my son, after going back to Metz to get him.

"I spent twelve years in the service of the King of Sardinia. I won't describe the mishaps I encountered there; they were countless. It's only by leaving France that one learns to miss it. Meanwhile my son was growing and showing great promise. I became acquainted in Turin with a French lady who had accompanied one of our princesses who married into that court. When this respectable lady took an interest in my misfortunes, I ventured to ask her to take my son to France so that he could finish his education there. I promised her that I would order my affairs well enough to be able to come and take him from her care in six years. She consented, took my poor child to Paris, spared no effort to give him a good upbringing, and regularly sent me news of him.

"I came a year earlier than I'd promised. I went to the lady's house, filed with the sweet expectation of embracing my son, of holding in my arms that token of a sentiment which I had betrayed, but which still burned in my heart . . . "Your son is no longer living," my worthy friend said to me with tears in her eyes. "He was a victim of the same passion that brought such unhappiness to his father. We'd taken him to the county. He fell in love there with a charming girl whose name I've sworn not to reveal. Carried away by the violence of his love, he tried to take by force what she'd refused him out of virtue . . . She stabbed him, intending only to frighten him, but she pierced his heart and he fell dead . . . "

At this point Madame de Courval fell into a kind of stupor which for a moment made the two men fear that she had suddenly lost her life. Her eyes were glazed, her pulse had stopped. Monsieur de Courval, who was all too clearly aware of the appalling way in which those deplorable events were related, told his son to be silent and hurried to his wife. She regained consciousness and said with heroic courage, "Let your son go on, monsieur. Perhaps I haven't yet reached the end of my afflictions."

Not understanding her sorrow over events that seemed to concern her only indirectly, but discerning something incomprehensible in her face, young Courval looked at her with emotion. Monsieur de Courval took his son's hand and, after distracting his attention from Florville, told him to go on with his story without dwelling on any unnecessary details, for it contained mysterious circumstances that were of the greatest interest.

"In despair over the death of my son," continued young Courval, "and no longer having anything to hold me in France--except you, father, but I didn't date to approach you and I dreaded your anger---I decided to travel to Germany . . . Ill-fated father, I still haven't told you the most painful part of my story," he said, wetting his father's hands with his tears. "I beg you to summon up your courage.

"When I arrived in Nancy I learned that a Madame Desbarres--this was the name my mother had adopted in her disorderly life, as soon as she had made you believe she was dead--had just been imprisoned for having stabbed her rival to death, and that she was perhaps going to be executed the next day."

"Oh, monsieur ! " exclaimed poor Florville, throwing herself in her husband's arms with tears and heart-rending cries. "Oh, monsieur, do you see the full extent of my afflictions?"

"Yes, madame, I see everything," said Monsieur de Courval, "but please let my son finish."

Florville restrained herself, but she had almost stopped breathing, all her feelings were impaired, and all her muscles were frightfully taut.

"Go on, my son, go on," said the unhappy father. "In a few minutes I'll explain everything to you."

"Well, monsieur," said young Courval, "I made inquiries to see if there was any confusion of names. I found that it was unfortunately all too true that the criminal was my mother. I asked to see her and my request was granted. I threw myself into her arms. 'I'm going to die guilty,' the poor woman said to me, 'but there's a terrible stroke of fate in the events that have led me to my death. A certain man was going to be suspected of my crime, and he would have been, because all the evidence was against him, but a woman and her two servants who happened to be in the inn saw me commit the murder, and I was so preoccupied that I didn't notice them. Their testimony was the sole cause of my death sentence. But no matter; I have only a little time left to talk to you, and I don't want to waste it on futile complaints. I have some important secrets to tell you; listen to them, my son.

"'As soon as my eyes are closed, go to my husband and tell him that among all my crimes there's one which he never knew, and which I finally confessed . . . You have a sister, Courval. She was born a year after you. I adored you and I was afraid she would be a drawback to you some day because your father might make a dowry for her by taking some of the money you would inherit. To keep it intact for you, I decided to get rid of my daughter and do everything in my power to make sure my husband would have no more children from our marriage. My disorders led me into other failings and forestalled the effect of those new crimes by making me commit other and more terrible ones; but as for my daughter, I mercilessly resolved to kill her. I was about to carry out that infamous plan, acting in concert with the wet nurse, whom I had amply compensated, when she told me that she knew a man who had been married for many years and constantly wanted children without being able to have them, and that she could rid me of my daughter without committing a crime, and in a way that might give her a happy life. I quickly accepted. That same night my daughter was left on the doorstep of that man with a note in her bassinet. As soon as I'm dead, hurry to Paris and beg your father to forgive me, not to curse my memory, and to claim his daughter for his own.'

"With these words, my mother kissed me and tired to calm the frightful agitation into which I'd been plunged by what she'd just told me . . . Father, she was executed the next day. Then a terrible illness nearly put me in my grave; for two years I hovered between life and death, with neither the strength nor the courage to write to you. The first use I've made of my recovered health has been to come and throw myself at your feet, to beg you to forgive my unfortunate mother, and to give you the name of the man who can tell you what has become of my sister: he's Monsieur de Saint-Prât."

Monsieur de Courval was deeply perturbed; all his senses were frozen, he nearly lost consciousness, his condition became alarming.

As for Florville, who had been torn to pieces for the past quarter of an hour, she stood up with the serenity of someone who had just come to a decision and said to Courval, "Well, monsieur, now do you believe that a more horrible criminal than the wretched Florville can exist anywhere in the world? Recognize me, Senneval, recognize me as your sister, the girl you seduced in Nancy, your son's murderer, your father's wife, and the infamous creature who led your mother to the scaffold . . . Yes, gentlemen, those are my crimes. When I look at either of you I see an object of horror; I either see my lover in my brother, or my husband in my father. And if I look at myself, I see only the abominable monster who stabbed her son and caused her mother's death. Do you think the Almighty can have enough torments for me? And do you think I can go on living any longer with the afflictions that are torturing my heart? No, I still have one more crime to commit, and it will avenge all the others."

The poor girl immediately leapt forward, snatched one of Senneval's pistols and shot herself in the head before either of the two men had time to realize her intention. She died without saying another word.

Monsieur de Courval fainted. His son, dazed by those horrible scenes, called for help as best he could. Florville no longer had any need for assistance: the shadows of death had already spread over her brow, and her features had been doubly contorted by the throes of despair and the upheaval of a violent death. She lay in a pool of her own blood.

Monsieur de Courval was carried to his bed. He was at death's door for two months. His son, in an equally painful state, was nevertheless fortunate enough to see his affection and care bring back his father's health. But after all the blows which fate had so cruelly rained down upon their heads, they decided to withdraw from the world. Austere solitude has taken them from their friends forever, and now, in the bosom of piety and virtue, each of them is peacefully finishing a sad and oppressive life which was given to him only to convince him, as well as those who will read this tragic story, that it is only in the darkness of the tomb that man can find the calm which the wickedness of his fellow man, the disorder of his passions, and, above all, the decrees of his fate, will always refuse to him on this earth.

www.ingramcontent.com/pod-product-compliance
Lightning Source LLC
Chambersburg PA
CBHW030415310726
48979CB00002B/427

* 9 7 9 8 8 8 0 9 0 4 7 3 0 *